THIS BOOK BELONGS TO

_____

MOMMY, IS IT KWANZAA YET?

Written by
Barbara Ann Johnson-Stokes, Esq.

Illustrated and Edited by
Jumaah I. Johnson

Baad Publishing Company
Cherry Hill, New Jersey

Picture Copyright © 2003 Jumaah I. Johnson
Text Copyright © 2003 Barbara Ann Johnson-Stokes, Esq.
Cherry Hill, New Jersey

Printed and Bound in the United States of America

ISBN 0-9725921-0-5

Library of Congress Control Number: 2002095650

Baad Publishing Company
P.O. Box 1234
Cherry Hill, NJ 08034-0034

First Printing December 2002

In loving memory of my beloved sister, Mary Ann Johnson.

Your sweet love and encouragement has carried me to be all that you knew I could be and all that I am.

Barbara Ann

Acknowledgements

Of course God, the most powerful from whom all things emanate is first to be recognized for making this book possible. Then follows my ancestors, whose struggle, blood, sweat and tears are on each page and in each word of this book. Dr. Maulana Karenga, the founder and creator of Kwanzaa. My husband, Edward Enessen Stokes, for his support of my efforts. Todd Weiss, for being there for the children. First Lady Nancy Reagan, whose wisdom concerning career and children helped me keep the value of my unborn children's lives in perspective. George Subira, author of <u>Black Folks Making Money in America</u>, who gave me direction regarding the self-publication of this book. All of my children's teachers and professors throughout their education.

Further thanks to the late Richard Hittleman, whose dedication to Hatha yoga helped me to complete this great project successfully, and my cousin Renee, her son Sean, Chris, Vince, Cehara and Julie Braswell, (Jumaah's third grade teacher) for reading the manuscript.

Finally, deep gratitude goes to long time family friend and graphic artist Eric Smith whose creativity, sincerity, and honesty completed the project with such wonderful design and imagination.

A Message to the Parents

Having been stripped of all sacred ways through slavery,

Having been stripped of all African tradition, with the exception of that which just could not be thrown away,

The remaining pieces have gathered together into the spirit and tradition of Kwanzaa.

I am grateful and have finally accepted the fact that it will never be the same as it was… before slavery.

Kujichagulia

Barbara Ann Johnson-Stokes, Esq.

MOMMY, IS IT KWANZAA YET?

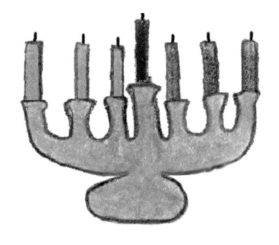

"It's Kwanzaa!" Jumaah thought while standing in her bedroom admiring herself in the mirror. She was wearing her mom's long, silver, African-style earrings, an African-style wrap on her head, a wrap-around skirt of beautiful African print, a dashiki top, and her brown school shoes. "This is different," thought Jumaah. "I am going to a Kwanzaa celebration for the first time!"

Jumaah was a kindergarten student at the Chad school. She was only four years old. She had a brother, Jawwaad, who also attended Chad school. He was five years old and in the first grade.

1

While Jumaah was admiring herself in the mirror, a frown suddenly appeared on her face. She thought, "I wonder where Dad and Jawwaad went."

Then, she remembered. "Oh, that's right, Dad took Jawwaad to Aunt Clara's house to get a dashiki to wear to the Kwanzaa celebration. I hope they hurry back!"

Jumaah then twisted away from the mirror in her bedroom. She yelled to her mom who was downstairs, baking a cake in the kitchen, with her baby brother, Jihsaan. "Mommy," Jumaah asked, "are Dad and Jawwaad back yet?" Her mom replied, "No, sweetheart, they will be here any minute now." 4

Jumaah began to smile bigger and brighter than ever. With great joy in her heart, she ran hurriedly down the blue-carpeted stairs and into the kitchen.

5

"Mmm, that smells so good!" exclaimed Jumaah. "I hope it tastes good," said her mom. "We are taking it to the Kwanzaa celebration at Chad School." "Mommy," Jumaah said, "is it Kwanzaa yet?"

"No, not really," replied her mom. "We are about to go to a Pre-Kwanzaa celebration at Chad school. You see, Kwanzaa begins on December 26th, the day after Christmas. It lasts for seven days, until the New Year, January 1st. Since no one attends Chad School during that time, it has a Pre-Kwanzaa celebration so that all of the children have a chance to experience the spirit of Kwanzaa together."

6

Jumaah listened closely to her mother. She then shouted, "Kujichagulia!" [koo-jee-chah-goo-LEE-ah] "Do you know what that means Mommy?" "Yes, Jumaah," replied her mom. "That is the Kwanzaa principle that means Self-determination."

"We learned that in school," said Jumaah. "We also learned six more principles, Mommy. Can I tell you all of them?" "Sure," said Jumaah's mom.

With her eyes big and bright and her brown skin looking shiny, soft and baby-like, Jumaah recited the seven principles of Kwanzaa for her mom.

"The first principle of Kwanzaa is Umoja [oo-MOH-jah], which means Unity. The second principle is the one I said before Mommy, Kujichagulia [koo-jee-chah-goo-LEE-ah]. It means Self-determination. The third principle of Kwanzaa, Ujima [oo-JEE-mah], means Collective work and responsibility. The fourth principle, Ujamaa [oo-JAH-mah], means Cooperative economics. The fifth principle, Nia [NEE-ah], means Purpose. The sixth principle of Kwanzaa, Kuumba [koo-OOM-bah], means Creativity. And guess what Imani [ee-MAH-nee], the seventh principle of Kwanzaa means, Mommy! Faith! My teacher told my class that one of these principles is remembered on each day of Kwanzaa by everyone in the family. Because they are so important, a candle that stands for that day's principle is lit during each of the seven days."

8

Just then, Jumaah thought she heard the front door open. "Hey!" she said, "I bet that's Dad and Jawwaad!" She quickly ran from the kitchen to the front door, but when she opened it, there was no one there.

She thought, "They should have come back from Aunt Clara's by now. I am going to call her house!"

9

Jumaah ran up the stairs faster than ever before. Her mom's silver earrings flopped up and down each time one of her little feet touched a stair step.

10

She ran into her mom's bedroom and grabbed the white telephone that was on the nightstand. "Now, let me see," she thought. "What is Aunt Clara's telephone number? Oh, I remember!" She dialed her number.

The telephone rang and rang, but Aunt Clara did not answer.

As her big eyes became filled with tears, she thought, "If Dad and Jawwaad do not get here soon, we are going to miss the Pre-Kwanzaa celebration. Mommy won't be able to take her cake!"

12

Just then, she heard the front door opening downstairs.

"Jumaah!" Jawwaad yelled. "Come see my dashiki!" She could not believe her ears!

13

As she ran from her mom's bedroom and down the stairway, one of her brown school shoes flew off her foot and rolled down the stairs, landing right at Jawwaad's feet. "Jawwaad!" she screamed. "Dad!" she yelled.

14

"Let's go celebrate Kwanzaa! Mommy, Jihsaan and I have all been waiting for you! Umoja!"

MOMMY, IS IT KWANZAA YET?
CROSSWORD PUZZLE

DOWN

1. Creativity

2. First African American Holiday

3. Cooperative Economics

4. A Country in Africa Beginning with "C"

5. Collective Work and Responsibility

ACROSS

1. Self-Determination

2. Unity

3. Faith

4. Purpose

Hint: Look for clues throughout the book!

ABOUT THE CHARACTERS

Jumaah Ingram Johnson (Illustrator, Editor)

As a child, Jumaah attended Chad School, located in Newark, New Jersey, for 2 years. She was approximately 3 years old when she began. While at Chad School, Jumaah was exposed to high academic standards as well as art and athletics, including gymnastics. At age 5, her test scores indicated that she was achieving on the second grade level. However, because Jumaah was so young, it was recommended by Chad School that she only skip one grade, and thus, she entered first grade at the young age of 5. After leaving Chad school, Jumaah continued to achieve academically and became a competitive gymnast.

On May 11, 2002, Jumaah graduated Magna Cum Laude from Ursinus College with a Bachelor of Science degree in Exercise and Sports Science at age 21. While attending Ursinus, she was on the Dean's List each semester and was featured in the 1999-2000 National Dean's List, an annually issued book honoring America's outstanding college students. She was also inducted into Phi Beta Kappa, the oldest and most prestigious National Honors Society, as well as Phi Epsilon Kappa, the Exercise and Sports Science Honors Society. Finally, Jumaah was accepted into Mensa, an international high IQ society.

Athletically, Jumaah competed for the Ursinus gymnastics team for 4 years, and she currently holds the school record for uneven bars with a score of 9.6. At the 2002 Division III National Gymnastics Championship, Jumaah placed first in the nation on the floor exercise with a two-day score of 19.20, as well as second in the nation in the all-around (37.35), fourth in the nation on the uneven bars (18.525) and fifth in the nation on the balance beam (19.25), a performance that earned her All-American honors in each of those events. Because of her excellence in gymnastics, she was named Most Valuable Player by her gymnastics coach and awarded the Ehret Prize for Excellence in Athletics by Ursinus College.

Jumaah has recently been accepted into a Physical Therapy Doctorate program at the University of Delaware. Because of her academic success, the University offered her a Presidential Fellowship, consisting of tuition and a stipend for the academic year.

In between her busy academic and athletic schedules, Jumaah found time to be the illustrator and editor for <u>Mommy, is it Kwanzaa Yet?</u> consistent with the Kwanzaa principles of Umoja (Unity) and Ujima (collective work and responsibility). Her creativity (Kuumba) and natural artistic ability brought to life a story based on her and her brother's first Kwanzaa celebration at Chad school.

Jawwaad Ingram Johnson (Publisher)

Jawwaad also attended Chad School for two years, and his test scores at Chad School revealed that he was also two grades ahead of his age group; he skipped one grade as well. Jawwaad developed such a strong interest in reading while at Chad School that he started reading encyclopedias at the age of 7. By the time he was 13, he was self-taught in the subject of geography and captured first place in the National Geographic Geography Contest at the schools that he attended in 7th and 8th grade. He developed in the sport of swimming during high school and furthered his capabilities on the swim team at William Patterson University. When he was 15, he used the skills he acquired as a swimmer to become a certified lifeguard for a private swim club. His lifeguard skills were tested on one occasion, when he rescued a child who had begun to drown.

Jawwaad attended William Patterson University for two years, during which he majored in History. Because of his strong academic ability, he was accepted into the History Honors program, and was honored by the Minority Students Academic Association for his academic achievement. Jawwaad then transferred to Pennsylvania State University where he continued his History major.

In addition to being a student-athlete, Jawwaad was also a soccer referee and the assistant soccer coach of his little brother's soccer team. The team won the championship game, defeating a team that had gone undefeated for a substantial period.

Recently, Jawwaad decided to delay his graduation in order to address his strong interest in entrepreneurship as a Network Business Center for the Matah, Network, an African American company organized and operating consistent with the Kwanzaa principle of Ujamaa (cooperative economics.) It is his belief that the time is now. Once he has stabilized this interest, he will return to school and attain his degree in History.

Consistent with the Kwanzaa Principles of Unity, (Umoja) Ujima, (collective work and responsibility) and Kuumba, (creativity) Jawwaad helped his mother create and name Baad (pronounced, Bod) Publishing Company, which will publish and distribute <u>Mommy, is it Kwanzaa Yet?</u>

Jihsaan Ingram Johnson (Assistant to the Publisher)

Jihsaan is the baby brother of Jumaah and Jawwaad. He will be a sophomore in high school in September of 2002. Jumaah and Jawwaad's positive influence has motivated him to achieve both academically and athletically. Jihsaan has developed into an independent thinker and an outspoken individual. He has been a self-taught Disc Jockey since the age of 12 and, since then, has been hired for numerous parties, his most challenging yet stimulating job being his mother and stepfather's wedding reception. Jihsaan is also an accomplished basketball player and has set becoming part of the NBA as one of his goals. Academically, he wants to become a doctor. When he returns to school in the Fall of 2002, Jihsaan will be taking all advanced level high school courses as well as a college-level history course.

Consistent with the Kwanzaa principle of Kuumba, (creativity), Jihsaan created the Kwanzaa Crossword puzzle for the book, after it was suggested by the graphic artist, Eric Smith.

Jihsaan will be active in the marketing and the distribution of <u>Mommy is it Kwanzaa Yet?</u> consistent with the Kwanzaa principles of Umoja, (Unity) and Ujima (collective work and responsibility).

Mommy (Author)

Barbara Ann Johnson-Stokes, Esq. is the mother of Jumaah, Jawwaad and Jihsaan. She is an attorney who presently practices in Lawnside, an African-American Community located in the southern region of New Jersey.

Consistent with the Kwanzaa principles of Kujichagulia, (Self-determination) Nia, (purpose) and Kuumba, (creativity), her deep concern for children all over the world and the need to communicate positive messages to them inspired her to write children's books and create Baad Publishing company.

Joseph Ingram Johnson (Father)

Joseph Ingram Johnson is the father of Jumaah, Jawwaad and Jihsaan. He passed away after a long illness. He was a business person and a Systems Analyst. Consistent with the Kwanzaa principles of Imani (Faith) and Umoja (Unity) he introduced Jumaah and Jawwaad to Chad school.

For further information and explanation of Kwanzaa, reference can be made to the book written by the creator of Kwanzaa, Dr. Maulana Karenga: <u>The African American Holiday of Kwanzaa: A Celebration of Family, Community and Culture</u>: Los Angeles, California, University of Sankore Press, 1988.